The Lost Princess

A Waves Crashing Novella

Nikki A Lamers

FREY DREAMS

For more information, address: freydreamspublications@gmail.com

First edition, October 2025

Editor, Dina Huessini

Cover Illustration & Design, Kris Wood

ISBN 978-1-951185-40-4 (paperback)

ISBN 978-1-951185-39-8 (ebook)

www.nikkialamersauthor.com

The Lost Princess

A WAVES CRASHING NOVELLA

Book 1

Nikki A Lamers

Chapter 1

The Beginning...

Ariana

Lightning flashes overhead, thunder booms echoing around me, blending with the sounds of the angry ocean as I swim, struggling to reach the surface. My head breaks through, my small body urgently gulping for air. Frantic, I look around, desperate to spot my mom and dad as our boat burns in the middle of the wide open waters, no land in sight.

Orange, red and yellow flames lick the stars, as if stealing all their wishes. My heart hammers against my ribcage, pounding louder than the raging storm surrounding me like it's attempting to consume me, while tears stream endlessly down my face. Thick, black smoke darkens the sky and the flames slowly begin to diminish, while remnants of what used to be our boat sinks into the murky waters as waves tug at my small frame, pulling me further away every second.

"Mom! Dad!"

Fins break the surface, flashing under the light of the fire and moon, circling the debris and inching closer. My breath catches as white hot fear takes hold of me, squeezing my lungs.

Sirens sound nearby drawing attention. Spotlights skim over the water, halting and immediately reversing back towards me.

The Coast Guard.

"Mom! Dad!" I scream into the darkness once again, my voice hoarse.

The Coast Guard boat cautiously approaches me, weaving through the wreckage, my heart sinking along with our boat.

Gasping for breath, my green eyes fly wide open, taking in the familiar surroundings of my bedroom decorated in shades of blue and green. Wiping my brow, I take a moment to calm my racing heartbeat from another nightmare. I've been having the same tragic dream since I was six years old, when I was found at sea. Mom and dad weren't so lucky.

Fortunately, I was adopted by wonderful parents who couldn't have kids of their own and grew up on a farm far from the water, my biggest fear.

I glance at my cell phone, my eyes widening at the time: 9:02 am. I'm late for class. Heaving a sigh, I lay back. It will be over before I get there anyway. It's not like it matters. As long as I turn in my thesis at the end of the semester, I'll likely still get my degree. My master's program is almost done and I'll be twenty-four in a week, yet I still don't know what I want to do with my life.

Knocking on my bedroom door startles me. "Ariana, are you up? It sounds like you're sleeping," my best friend and roommate Saylor, calls through the door.

"Good morning to you too. I didn't know you acquired x-ray vision."

"Arie," she says my name in warning.

"Yes, I'm up, I'm up, but I can't believe I'm late!"

"Late for spring break?"

My shoulders relax as I breathe a sigh of relief knowing I didn't miss class. In the next moment, I remember what this week will entail and I frown. "Right. The beach. I'm getting ready."

"Good, because we have to leave for the beach house soon to meet everyone. Since I have the key, we can't be late."

Groaning, I bite back the refusal that wants to spill from my mouth. It's about time I get over my fear. I can't live my life terrified of the ocean. Besides, I don't have to go in the water or even anywhere near it. Taking a deep breath, I push my inky black hair out of my face and sit up. "Yeah, I know. I'll be ready. Promise."

Her heavy sigh of relief echoes through the door. "Okay, good. Thanks. I'll start packing a cooler."

"We can always stop at the store if we need to," I remind her before she walks away, forcing myself to get out of bed.

An hour later I'm packed, showered, and dressed in a simple teal green sundress with spaghetti straps and silver flip flops. I pull my long hair into a ponytail before locking up while Saylor waits in the driveway. Tossing my bag in the back, I slide into the passenger seat.

She grins. "You're not only ready, but you're living dangerously."

My eyebrows draw down in confusion making her laugh. "By coming to the beach?"

She shakes her blonde head, her familiar purple streak falling in front of her soft, brown eyes. "Your shoes."

"I may be clumsy, but even I can't fall while sitting in your car."

She giggles. "And you are actually sitting in my car to come to the beach. I thought for sure you were going to back out on me."

I wince, knowing I almost did just that. "I'm sorry I gave you reason to doubt me, but there's no way I was going to back out of it this year. I promised you we would celebrate our birthdays together before we graduate."

She squeals. "And we're going to have so much fun! I know you're going to love being out on the Cape."

My heart thrums, nervous energy running through my body, hoping she's right. Tuning out my doubts, I turn up the radio and sing along, Saylor joining in.

Just before we reach the beach house, she turns down the music and takes a deep breath, her hands wringing the steering wheel. "So..." she mumbles, dragging out the word, her cheeks flushing. "There's kinda something I need to tell you."

My stomach plummets and I force myself to keep my words light. "Your post went viral and now you're worth millions."

A nervous giggle escapes her lips. "I wish." She stops at the only light in the small Massachusetts beach town and rubs her hands along her short skirt, not even glancing in my direction.

"What's wrong, Saylor? You're making me nervous."

"Well, we kinda have more people coming than we talked about this week."

"What's *kinda* more company?" My nerves churn in my gut, becoming their own tidal wave and causing chaos to my insides. Saylor's other friends are not my favorite people. Then again, I'm not exactly theirs either, especially when it comes to Cleo.

"The boys are coming with Freddie," she starts, mentioning her twin brother. He's the masculine version of her when it comes to looks, but he's much taller, barely over six feet, light brown hair, and eyes. "That includes my cousin, Kai," she taunts wiggling her eyebrows.

I've never met her cousin, but I've seen pictures, and she knows I think he's hot. Who wouldn't? He's six-foot-two with brown hair, lightened from the sun, violet eyes I imagine are more incredible in person and a smile that makes me melt. "I knew your twin brother was coming with Charlie and Atlas. It's his birthday too and they're nice guys."

"Yeah..."

"And doesn't your cousin, Kai, live out here?" She nods, biting her lip. "I don't even know him. Why would I be mad?"

"Who said you were going to be mad?"

My eyes widen and I cross my arms over my chest. "You, when you started strangling the steering wheel to its demise."

She heaves a sigh halting her movements as she presses the gas. "I'm not doing that."

I huff a laugh, arching my eyebrows in challenge. "Saylor..."

"Okay, fine, I am," she admits, throwing her hands up in frustration. "Cleo and Lola are going to be there too," she spits out, staring at the road as if she's struggling to see out the windshield when it's nothing but blue skies and sunshine besides the traffic.

"Ugh," I groan, my head falling back against the seat. "Why? I can deal with Lola, but Cleo?" This weekend might be worse than I thought.

She opens her mouth to respond. "Arie–"

I smack the dashboard, halting her words. "Don't answer that. It won't do me any good and I'll be fine."

Sighing, she turns towards the water. "I'm sorry I didn't tell you sooner, but in the past, you never said yes. I didn't want you to back out before we even got here."

"I wouldn't do that to you." My stomach turns as the lie falls from my tongue. Cleo being here changes everything.

"Thanks, but my point is, I'm glad you're here."

She glances at me and I force a smile. "This weekend is about us. It's fine."

The sound of the ocean becomes louder, drawing our attention. My chest tightens and my fingers tingle as I look out at the water. Nightmares linger on the edge of my sanity. Trying to keep them at bay, I attempt to focus on the positives, if there are any.

"Isn't it beautiful?" she questions, her voice filled with awe.

Sun glitters off the blues and greens of the ocean. The water rocks back and forth, waves rising, cresting, and crashing into the rocky and sandy shores of the coast. Power emanates from every droplet working together to form a beast in every wave. All the monsters collaborate, wreaking havoc prompted by pure evil living in the unseen world underneath the surface. That same evil ripped my parents away from me. It's not something I will ever forget, but voicing my fear only makes me question my sanity or prompts others to urge me to respect the ocean.

Respect is not the issue.

"I'm not sure if beautiful is the word I would use, but it sure is something," I mumble under my breath, staring at the cacophony in front of us.

"You're going to love it here, Ari, I just know it." Saylor continues, ignoring my comment as she pulls into a long cobblestone driveway.

A massive white beach house with a wraparound porch comes into view on our left. We pass by a beautifully manicured front lawn and gardens before reaching a circle drive in front of the house. A white stone fountain adorned with two mermaids, their tails curled together sits in the middle of the circle as we pull around, parking in front of the steps. The glass entry door gives me a view through the middle of the house, all the way to the back and out to the ocean.

"Wow. Maybe I won't even run into Cleo in that thing," I murmur, hopeful.

She rolls her eyes, giggling. "It will be fun."

"Saying it more will not make it true," I tease, but unable to hold back my grin.

"Come on. Let's unpack and pick your room before everyone else gets here."

My eyes widen as we climb out of the car, grabbing our bags. "I get my own room?"

"Of course. I'd like to find a man this week and bring him around without having to kick you out of our room."

"Okay. Just don't put me anywhere near Cleo and you won't find yourself homeless and without a best friend." She laughs, but we both know I'm serious–maybe.

Chapter 2

Kai

I'm finally going to meet the girl I've heard so much about. Well, I guess she's a woman now. And from the pictures I've seen on Saylor's social, she's gorgeous with her dark hair, striking green eyes, button nose and curves that drive me wild. Seeing her for the first time...damn. I cannot wait.

My only hesitation is my mom. With any luck, she won't realize who I'll be introduced to this weekend. Pressure from her is the last thing I need.

Lifting the green comforter, I swipe my bag from underneath my white coral bed. I grab mostly shorts and t-shirts from my matching dresser before finding what I need from my bathroom, maintaining the protective bubble around it all to keep it dry.

Quietly, I sneak out the back door of my bedroom, trying to make my way out of my dad's stone castle. Slinging my waterproof duffle bag over my shoulder, I look around, hoping I won't be spotted.

"Your majesty," a deep voice calls a moment before I'm able to escape.

Startling, I spin around, my wide eyes landing on two of my good friends as I exhale a sigh of relief. "Henry, Seb, what the hell? And cut the majesty crap."

"If the crown fits…" Henry shrugs brushing his blond hair out of his eyes.

Sebastian, Henry's opposite at first glance with black hair and a dark complexion, smirks, watching through his golden gaze, non-apologetic. "Where are you sneaking off to?"

"I'm headed to the surface to hang out at my cousins' place for the week."

"If you're talking about Saylor, I'm in," Henry announces, wiggling his eyebrows.

With a shove he falls back, laughing and snapping his emerald, green fin to catch his balance. "Freddie will be there," I tell him knowing they aren't each other's biggest fan, likely because Henry is always hitting on Saylor, Freddie's twin sister.

Instantly, his face falls. "I'm out."

Chuckling, I offer him breadcrumbs. "If we have a bonfire on the beach, I'll be sure to let you guys know."

Sulking, he grumbles, "Sure."

"Sounds good to me," Sebastian agrees, flipping his evergreen tail. "Your dad knows you're leaving?"

"He knows where I'll be."

"So, that's why you're slinking out through the escape door." Henry nods in understanding, giving me a crooked grin.

I shake my head, not bothering to respond. They know my dad attempts to control everything I do and trouble tends to find me and my cousins when we hang out at the beach house. Perception of our community is everything to him. My mom, on the other hand, wants me to be networking with the right people. Unfortunately, we don't see eye to eye on who those people are.

"I gotta go. I'll catch up with you guys later," I tell them before I swim away, my navy blue and dark purple tail flipping behind me kicking up sand, leaving them and my dad's oceanic kingdom deep on the sea floor in my wake.

Bypassing the colorful stone wall of the town of Pierrecel, filled with a mix of magical ethnicities, history, and tradition, I kick and exit a cave hidden in the base of a rocky cliff near Freddie and Saylor's place.

Slipping through the magical barrier, I swim towards the shore with a deep breath, a twist and a flip. My mind settles, and my fin swiftly transforms to two legs, wearing green swim shorts, my kick remaining strong. Shaking my head, water sprays around me as I stride out of the ocean. Saltwater drips into my eyes and I wipe it away, the distinct scent of old seaweed causing my nose to wrinkle. Walking across the sand towards the beach house, I look up at the wall of windows along the back of the house, devoid of any movement.

Climbing up the steep back stairs, I yell as I approach, "Freddie? Saylor? You here?"

I step through the back door and drop my duffel on the white tile floor, opening my mouth to call out again just as a raven-haired beauty rounds the corner into the large, open, modern kitchen halting my footsteps. My insides tingle with anticipation at the sound of her soft gasp. My gaze runs over her full lips, round breasts, narrow waist, and wide hips, perfect to grasp when she wraps her long legs around me.

Damn, I want that to happen.

She clears her throat, her pale skin pink and blotchy. Her wide, captivating bright green eyes hold me hostage.

She squeaks, a choked sound leaving her lips. Her hands are at her throat, while she looks at me in despair and it hits me. "Are you choking?" I ask, rushing towards her. She nods frantically as I wrap her in my arms from behind. Ignoring the sudden jolt of electricity running through me, I place my fist below her sternum and my other hand over it, jerking in and up, a grape dislodging from her throat and landing in the sink.

Coughing ensues, my shoulders sagging with relief. I spin her around, cupping her face in my hands as I check her over, my fingers prickling with the simple touch. "Are you okay?"

"Yeah," she rasps, nodding. "Thank you."

I'm an asshole. She's choking while I stare at every inch of her, imagining fucking her. "No more grapes for you. I'm Kai."

She gives me a small smile, the simple gesture making my heart skip a beat, my skin tingling everywhere we touch. My body feels like it's coming alive for the first time, my senses on high alert. "Hi, Kai. I'm Ariana. Some people call me Arie."

"Ariana...I've heard a lot about you. I'm happy to finally meet you." Her cheeks flush, her green eyes sparkling, accelerating my heartbeat. I could easily get lost in her.

"Well, isn't this sweet," Cleo croons, her sarcasm thick on her tongue as she steps into the kitchen, her red hair pulled up into a ponytail. Lola steps in right behind her, her long blonde hair hanging over her shoulders in matching braids.

My body stiffens. Cleo is the last person I want to see. Guess I should've known she might be here. I grit my teeth, slowly letting my hands drop to my sides, instantly feeling the loss. Forcing a polite smile, I greet them. "Hey, Cleo. Lola."

Cleo focuses on me, a broad smile lighting up her face as she slips in front of Ariana, throwing her arms around me and kissing me on the lips like she has every right. My eyes widen as I firmly push her back, but I shouldn't be surprised. Sometimes I wonder how I ever dated Cleo. It didn't take long for me to see the ugly side of her, but I question how I overlooked it in the first place. Unfortunately, she hasn't left me alone since. Can't she take a hint?

"I missed you, Kai."

"That makes one of us," I grumble, showing my irritation.

Ariana huffs a laugh and covers her mouth, pretending to cough. Apparently we have a similar opinion of Cleo bringing a small smile to my face. I like Arie already.

"Don't be an ass, Kai. We're going to be together all week. If you're good, maybe we can have some fun together like we used to." She wiggles her eyebrows suggestively.

"No thanks. I do just fine without you, Cleo." She glares at me, but I ignore her, turning to Lola. "So, Lola, do you know Arie?"

She smiles, nodding. "Yeah, we went to high school together." Courteously, she glances at her and waves. "Hi, Arie."

"Hi." Ariana pastes a smile on her face, the look anything but genuine and points behind her. "I'm going to go find Saylor."

"No need, I'm right here," she announces, Freddie, Charlie, and Atlas right behind her, all part of our underwater kingdom. "Put a shirt on Kai."

"But it's nice out and we're at the beach," I argue. Saylor's eyes narrow making me laugh. "Yeah, yeah. Your house, your rules. Hey, guys." I grin, greeting my friends. "What's up?"

"Kai! Hey man, good to see you." Atlas grins, giving me a slight head nod, his light brown hair longer than it was the last time I saw him.

I tip my head towards him, pulling a black t-shirt from my duffle bag and over my head. "It's been a while."

"Yeah, my dad has had me training at the castle," Atlas explains, pursing his lips.

"A castle?" Ariana echoes, arching her eyebrows in question.

Startled, Atlas shakes his head. "That's just what I call the place my dad works at. He's an advisor for some big shot family and he had me interning there this summer with him." Knowing he's been spending time at my parents' place tells me how much I've been avoiding it when I can.

"Oh, like a political advisor?" she asks.

"Something like that," Atlas agrees, his gaze swinging to mine, searching for a subject change. "What about you?"

"His dad has been trying to entice him into the family business," Charlie claims, before I have a chance to respond, unknowingly sharing more than I'd like. Charlie's dad is the head of my family's security and hears things I wish he didn't. He looks the same with his dark brown hair cut close to his head and his brown eyes mischievous.

"It's no big deal. He's just been keeping me busy helping out. I'm not sure what I'm doing yet. What are the plans for tonight?" I redirect.

"We thought we could hike up the cliff down the beach with some drinks and snacks for the sunset," Freddie states.

Saylor frowns, tapping the back of her twin's blond head in annoyance. "Not just snacks, I put together a charcuterie board, a fruit and veggie platter and everything."

Freddie chuckles, holding his hands up in surrender. "Sorry."

Charlie steps up behind her, giving her a hug and pressing his lips to her temple. "And it looks amazing, babe."

I arch my eyebrows in surprise. "You two?"

"Are nothing," Saylor claims, pinching her lips tightly together and giving Charlie a pointed look. She steps away and busies herself gathering food while Freddie grabs beer, wine, and seltzers, packing it in a cooler backpack.

"Got it." I nod, taking in Charlie's look of betrayal as he slithers away. Interesting. This week could reveal more than I expected. "The cliff sounds good to me. Is everyone in?" Agreements sound from around the room as we all help put some things together before we leave. My gaze constantly shifts to Arie, desperate to know more about her.

Looks like it will be a fascinating weekend.

Chapter 3

Ariana

Wow. I can't take my eyes off him.

Kai doesn't only have a killer smile and eyes like I've never seen before, but his body is all lines and ridges of hard muscle. And of course, I had to go and pop a grape in my mouth before finding him standing in the kitchen, shirtless, making me choke so he had to save me.

Ugh. Why me?

At least Saylor was able to talk to her brother and come up with a plan I'm comfortable joining. Giving her another grateful smile, I breathe a sigh of relief knowing I won't be the only one on dry land. At least not today. My focus strays from the ground and I stumble over a rock. A hand wraps around my waist and pulls me upright, my back to his front. "The trails can be rough. Be careful. I wouldn't want you to get hurt," Kai whispers in my ear.

"Thank you, Kai. I'm fine," I insist, stepping away from him and forcing myself to keep moving forward. "I'm a little clumsy sometimes." I peek back at him, watching his reaction.

"Glad you're okay." His lips quirk up, looking at me like he wants to say more, but he lets it slide.

"So, Arie," Cleo begins, spitting my name with distaste, "why did you decide to grace us with your presence this time? I was kinda hoping you'd flake like you always do." She glares in my direction as we all hike up the trail of rocks, grass and sand, making our way towards the top of the cliff.

Pressing my lips tightly together, I don't respond, knowing anything coming out of my mouth would be the opposite of cordial. The scent of saltwater and sand fills my senses, redirecting my focus and making me restless.

"It's our birthday, Cleo. I'm glad she's here. If you have a problem with it and you can't grow up and be nice, you can leave," Saylor challenges, narrowing her eyes.

Cleo scoffs. "But Saylor–"

A smile tugs at my lips, thankful for my best friend while I tune out Cleo's excuse. Her words hold no weight with me.

"It's your birthday too?" Kai asks, tilting his head to the side, curious.

"Yeah. My birthday is the day before Saylor and Freddie, March 17th. I promised Saylor I'd come this year so we could celebrate together before we graduate again."

"Ah. St. Patrick's Day."

"Yeah. That always keeps it interesting."

"I'm sure. I assume you're also going to be twenty-four since I know you two were college roommates?" He arches his brow in question.

My stomach flips, loving that he knows something about me, even if it's small and technically also about his cousins. Internally, I roll my eyes at my excitement over my small win. Maybe I'm the one who needs to grow up, but being around Cleo makes me feel like I'm that clumsy, awkward, girl in high school all over again and I hate it. I refuse to let her get to me.

Nodding, I reply, "Yup. And we're still living together while we finish up our masters' programs."

"Well, this is going to be fun," he claims, grinning wide, and sending chills down my spine.

"I think so too," I whisper, lightheaded. "What do you want to do for your birthday? Like what are some of your favorite things to do?"

Not expecting the question, I shrug, thinking. "I don't know. Hiking and taking pictures for fun, but I haven't really been able to do those things many places. I haven't traveled much."

"Because you're content in the middle of nowhere all by yourself. You don't need friends when you have the animals on the farm," Cleo comments, laughing.

"Stop listening in on other people's conversations," Kai demands, shaking his head. "This isn't high school."

"I just happened to hear because I wanted to talk to you, Kai," Cleo says, her whining already getting on my nerves.

"Well, I'm talking to Arie."

"Sorry to interrupt," she says, giving him a look of regret, and taking me by surprise. I've never heard her apologize for anything.

"Did you bring your camera?" Kai questions, returning his gaze to me. "You will love this view. I'm sure the pictures would be stunning."

"Not this time. It's just back at the house. I know it's not the same, but I have my phone." He nods in understanding. "What about you? What do you like to do?"

His eyes widen. "Me? I love being outside, but I guess I mostly swim, surf, dive–basically anything to do with the water and I'm there."

"So, the opposite of me." My lips twitch up in amusement.

"Don't you know opposites attract?" My cheeks heat. He chuckles, the sweet sound making it difficult to catch my breath.

"Let's see, I love hiking too, but it's the view of the water that really gets me. The ocean has a unique beauty you don't find anywhere else in the world. Well, mostly," he adds gazing into my eyes. My heart skips a beat as he looks at me like he's seeing into my soul.

Goosebumps erupt on my skin. Taking a deep breath, I break his stare and quickly shake off the intensity, exhaling slowly. Attempting to ignore his compliment, I arch my eyebrows in challenge. "You're right, but it also has a power that doesn't exist anywhere else." That fact alone terrifies me.

"No truer words have been spoken, but I would keep you safe." He grins, his eyes sparkling with mischief. "Maybe I could entice you to come in the water with me. I promise I would take care of you."

Ironically, I think I believe him. My heart races and I lick my lips, wanting to agree, but my fear holds me back once again. "I'm..." We reach the top, the view grabbing my attention as I trail off. "Wow," I mumble under my breath.

Cautiously, I approach the edge to take it all in. The jagged edges of the rocks carve out the land below me with a few soft patches of grass amongst the stone. The sun shines bright, red, orange, yellow and purple remain prominent over the blues and greens of the ocean where they meet at the horizon. A few sailboats, two motorboats and a huge tanker disturb the calm, cutting through the water. The sandy beach rises towards the rocks with people enjoying the last of the sun before it's swallowed up by sea and sky.

Tall seagrass and colorful flowers sit at the base on one side, the other side disappearing into the rocks.

"It's stunning," I whisper, my declaration taking me by surprise.

"You can say that again," Kai murmurs, stepping up next to me, smiling. His small gesture slows my heartrate, calming me, the opposite of how I thought I would feel the closer I got to the ocean. "It's incredible, isn't it?"

I glance at him out of the corner of my eye and quickly return my gaze to the view. "Definitely. I have to come back up here and bring my camera."

"I'll come along when you do."

"Really?"

His broad grin lights up his face, momentarily taking my breath away. "Of course. I'd love to do this with you."

Smiling, I nod in agreement, butterflies taking over my insides. "Okay, I'd like that."

"Awesome. Why don't we make a day of it? We'll come up here so you can take pictures and then you'll come in the water with me."

My breath hitches. "I...I don't know," I stammer, causing me to realize I'm actually considering it. What the hell am I thinking? Is it because it's Kai asking me? How can he already make me feel safe? I don't know him, not really. Or am I truly ready to tackle my fear of the water?

"The invitation remains open for you. When you're ready, we'll do it, together." Tilting his head to the side, he gives me a crooked grin, causing my insides to twist into knots once again.

"I'm surprised you're so close to the edge," Saylor comments as she turns to me on my other side, pulling my attention.

Blushing, I glance in her direction. "It really is a gorgeous view and it's not like I'm afraid of heights."

"No, but we all know you're afraid of water," Cleo proclaims, a wicked grin on her face making my stomach churn. Turning to her, I narrow my eyes, attempting to read her intent a moment too late. Before anyone has a chance to react, she closes the distance between us and plants her hands on my shoulders, shoving me hard.

Gasping, I fall back, losing my footing. My eyes go wide, and my arms flail, trying to grab onto anything as her laughter echoes around me. Before I even catch my breath to scream, my body hits the cold water, jolting me like a shockwave. The water swiftly consumes me, ensnaring me in its clutches and dragging me under. The feeling of floating hits me, saltwater overtaking my senses as my panic sets in and my world spins out of control.

Chapter 4

Kai

My heart stops, my reflexes too slow as I reach out for Ariana. Unfortunately, I'm not able to do anything, but watch her fall over the edge, her terror palpable.

"What the fuck is wrong with you?" I challenge, scowling. Ripping my shirt off, I toss it to the side along with my phone and kick off my shoes, diving off the cliff without waiting for a response, the shrill sound of Cleo's voice trailing after me.

My body plunges into the icy water, fin instantly flipping out behind me as I race towards Ariana, desperate to find her, protect her. I spin in a circle, attempting to judge where she went under, barely able to focus on the sounds around me. My heart thrashes against my ribcage while my eyes scan the water. Diving a little deeper, I continue searching, my anger and distress growing by the second. I have to find her. She needs to be okay.

Finally, spotting some unusual movement, I dive closer. Ariana's dark hair floats around her with her head spinning, looking erratically around as if not sure which direction will take her to the surface. Inching towards her, I watch helplessly as she slips deeper into the depths of the ocean as if something is pulling her under, her body already giving up without a fight. I won't let that happen.

The moment she sees me, her eyes widen to the size of saucers, her green orbs showing me both her relief and her panic, urging me to swiftly close the distance between us. I push harder, refusing to let the currents take me anywhere but towards Ariana. Her head wobbles just as I reach her. She's likely dizzy, about to pass out from lack of oxygen.

Fuck.

Lurching forward, I grasp her under the arms and pull her towards me, knowing she's not safe yet. I don't want our first kiss to be this way, but I have no choice if I'm going to save her. Cradling her face in my hands, I look into her eyes, holding her gaze, begging her to trust me. She nods, hopefully understanding my silent plea. Blinking slowly, one more bubble slips out from between her lips letting me know she's almost out of air.

I'm out of time.

Without another thought, I press my lips to hers, my heartbeat skyrocketing as I seal our mouths together and breathe air into her lungs. She tastes sweet like strawberry wine with a hint of something I can't place. I push the thought away, reminding myself I need to keep her safe. I'm doing this to save her. This kiss isn't about us.

Keeping our mouths sealed, I weave one hand into her hair and wrap my other arm around her waist, drawing her into me. My body groans, desperate to get her even closer, but I need her in the right state of mind for that, and this isn't it. Holding tight, I snap my hips, flipping my fin, and pushing us towards the surface, away from our friends. Sliding through the magical barrier, I guide us inside the cave at the base of the cliff to give us privacy. Hopefully giving her space will help so she can deal with what just happened and everything about to come to fruition after all these years.

As we near the surface, her mouth starts to move against mine. A soft moan escapes her lips, and I respond in kind, no longer able to hold myself back. My tongue slides inside her mouth, tasting, exploring, and connecting with hers. Nearly forgetting where we are, I quickly get lost in our kiss, every part of me on fire even in these icy waters.

Her hands fall to my chest, roaming and burning a trail in her wake across my skin. Our kiss goes deeper, her tongue pushing into mine, twisting, licking, making my already hardened length turn to granite. My entire body burns, vibrating with desire and anticipation.

Damn, I want her.

Our heads break the surface, startling us both and giving her a cold dose of reality. She rips her mouth away from mine and shoves me away just before my legs come under me. Her eyes widen, another gasp escaping her lips as she stumbles back into the water, quickly getting her legs underneath her while her shoes begin sinking into the wet sand.

The look she gives me no longer holds fear, but her confusion remains. "Kai?" she questions, her voice trembling.

Cautiously stepping closer, I reach out, running my hand tenderly over her hair, and holding her stare. Taking a deep breath, I keep my voice calm, and try to reassure her. "Yes, it's me, Kai. You're okay, Arie."

She shakes her head in denial, her eyes flitting over my body to the water and back, her breathing quickly becoming rapid once again. "No, no, no..."

"Breathe, Ariana. You're going to make yourself pass out. Please, just breathe. It's okay. You're going to be okay," I emphasize as she stumbles backwards into the water.

Her eyes roll back and they flutter closed, her body immediately going limp. "Ariana!" Reaching out, I wrap my arm around her waist, catching her a moment before her head sinks below the surface once again. With a heavy sigh, I scoop her up into my arms, holding her close. Her head rests on my chest, just over my heart, our bodies seeming to be in sync as I stride towards the beach. My skin tingles with awareness every spot our bodies connect making me wonder if it's lust, or if maybe we're meant to be together. I've never believed in any of that shit before, but there's something different igniting between us that I sure as hell can't explain.

But I crave it.

I crave her.

My mother flashes in my mind, disrupting my thoughts and making me frown. She's relentless about controlling the prophecy. What if she's right? What if everything I've ever heard about the lost princess and the prophecy is true?

We could all be fucked. Then again, I've heard so many different versions. Which one is real? If any?

Finding a spot, hidden by most, I make my way across the shore. Carefully, I lay her down on the sand and stretch out right beside her. My eyes glide over her curves, relaxing as I watch the rise and fall of her chest. Knowing she's breathing on her own, I let my mind and gaze drift, settling on her sweet, kiss-swollen lips.

Damn, I want to kiss her again, but I want to make sure she knows what she's doing this time. I'm not quite sure that was the case in the water. Although my lips sealed over hers, she kissed me first. But did she realize what was happening? Did she think she was dreaming? If that's true, I want to be part of every single one of her dreams. My lips twitch, tingling at the thought, my body coming alive.

Taking a deep breath, I attempt to calm my head and heart. I'm not sure if I'm going to be much help if this is the way my body wants to react around her. I won't be able to keep my head on straight with my body leading the way. There's no denying I want her and the chemistry—damn. I feel the surge of electricity vibrating between us. She's already someone I don't want to say no to, for any reason. That's not good, especially if the stories we heard growing up are not just fairytales.

"Fuck," I mutter under my breath. I'm confident this woman is going to be trouble for me—hopefully not to my demise.

Staring at the beautiful woman lying beside me, the sound of her soft breaths remains slow and steady, the only thing keeping me calm. She will be okay.

Irregular splashing draws my attention. Henry and Sebastian surface, both shaking their heads to rid their hair of water.

"Kai, what the hell are you doing here?" Seb questions. "Your parents are pissed you took off. They came looking for you."

I quirk my brow. "They did? Together?"

Sebastian shrugs. "Well, your mom was pissed. Your dad was mostly annoyed you left earlier than he expected."

"Did you tell them where I went?"

"Yeah, but we thought you were staying at your cousins' place," Henry adds. "Guess there's no bonfire tonight."

"Looks like you'll have to wait to hit on Saylor." Sebastian smirks.

Henry rolls his eyes and stalks out of the water towards me. Instinctively, I scoot a little closer to Arie. "Who's she?"

"Off limits," I speak, my voice low and commanding.

Both their eyes widen and they gingerly step closer. "Is she all right?" Sebastian asks.

Glancing at her, I heave a sigh. "She will be. I think she was just in shock. Cleo pushed her off the cliff and she's afraid of water, so I jumped in after her."

"What the hell is wrong with that girl?" Sebastian mumbles under his breath.

"She's a jealous bitch," Henry states making all of us laugh.

"I still can't believe she did that. I'm just glad I found her when I did."

"Did she see your fin?" Sebastian inquires.

My lips pinch tightly together and I nod my head in affirmation.

"Who is she?" Henry repeats.

"Saylor's roommate and best friend."

"She's been living with her for all these years? Damn, she's gorgeous," Sebastian mutters. I shove his shoulder and he crashes into the sand, laughing. "What is she to you, Kai?"

"Just Arie. We met when I got to the house."

"Sure, that's all she is?" Sebastian asks, his tone laced with doubt.

"No," I answer honestly, running my hand through my hair in frustration. "I'm interested, but... I think she's the woman I've been hearing about for years and I have no idea what the fuck to do about it."

"Shit," they mumble at the same time.

"Yeah," I mutter, dropping my hand to my side once again.

After a beat of silence, Henry asks, "Do you need anything? We're heading into town."

"Nah, thanks anyway. When she wakes up, I'll bring her into town to get her something to eat. I'm just going to keep an eye on her until then." I glance over at her, awed by her beauty and anxious to have her captivating green eyes on mine once again.

"Okay. We'll see you later man," Sebastian says, both him and Henry waving as they walk away.

My gaze quickly averts back to Arie, and I brush a loose lock of dark hair away from her pale face, tucking it behind her ear. "Please wake up, Arie. I need you to wake up for me," I plead softly, wondering if she hears me. I only pray you don't panic about what you saw when you awaken.

Chapter 5

Ariana

My eyes blink open and instantly shut, startled by the deep violet eyes shining down on me, eyes that feel like they see into my soul.

Kai.

He's really here. My heart thrums inside my chest, my fingers twitching, wanting to reach for him to know if he's truly there, but I don't. Maybe I'm losing my mind. Either that or I just had one hell of a dream, one I don't want to wake up from.

But he's here in this reality.

Forcing my eyes open once again, I squint into the sunlight, my gaze traveling over Kai's shirtless form, wearing nothing but green shorts, his long, firm, tan legs stretching out beside me causing my heart to lurch. His legs, not a tail or a fin.

"You're awake." He grins, giving me goosebumps.

Nodding, I stare at him, trying to process what happened. When I saw him in the water, he had a fin like a mermaid or merman, whatever the term would be.

Did I imagine that? "Yeah. What happened?"

He clenches his jaw, taking a calming breath. "Cleo pushed you and you fell off the cliff into the ocean."

"So that did happen." Heaving a sigh, I frown.

He grinds his teeth, letting out a slow breath. "Yeah. It did. I'm sorry she did that to you."

"We've never been fans of each other. It's not your fault." He arches his eyebrows, giving me a look, letting me know he doesn't agree with me. "So, how long ago did you two date?"

He groans, running his hand through his hair and dropping it to his side. "Over five years ago, but it's one of my biggest regrets."

My eyes widen in shock, remembering her kissing him in the kitchen. "Five years and she's still like that?"

He makes a face. "Yeah. It was at the end of my freshman year of college. She convinced me she had changed, but it wasn't long before her true colors were shining like a beacon once again. The attention she gives me goes in waves. Do we have to talk about her?"

"Sorry."

"It's okay, she's just not my favorite subject."

"Mine either," I concede.

He grimaces and stares out at the water before looking back at me. Tilting his head to the side, he studies me. "Do you remember anything else?"

"I didn't know how to reach the surface. It felt like my lungs were going to explode. I was terrified, but you saved me, again."

"Ariana, I wouldn't have let anything happen to you, but I have to ask...why does the water scare you so much?"

My cheeks flush, my gaze falling to my lap. Surprising myself, I tell him the truth. "When I was little, I was in an accident with my mom and dad. I don't remember much about what happened, but I remember being in the water crying, looking for them when the Coast Guard found me in the ocean." I press my lips tightly together as a wave of emotion hits me. Gulping hard, I continue, "My parents were never found. I was adopted by wonderful parents, but I still have nightmares about that night."

Reaching out, he grabs my hand, squeezing. The small gesture presses against my heart and soothes my soul. "I'm so sorry you went through that, Ariana. No one should have to, especially so young, but I'm really glad you told me."

I offer him a small smile. "Me too."

The corners of his lips tug up. "You know, I could help you get comfortable with the water again. Maybe it would take away your nightmares."

He might be right, but even coming on this trip wasn't easy. Not ready to answer, I take a deep breath and change the subject. "Thank you for jumping in after me. I wouldn't be alive if it weren't for you."

Reaching out, he brushes my hair back. "I'm just glad you're okay." Clearing his throat, he moves back and arches his eyebrows in challenge. "Remember anything else?"

A blush creeps up my neck, coloring my cheeks, recalling the way his lips felt against mine—soft, sweet and confident. "You kissed me."

His grin broadens and his body sinks into the sand, seeming to relax as if those are the words he has been waiting for. "Well, you started it."

My eyebrows draw down in confusion, remembering it differently. "No, that's not..." I trail off, searching his eyes for confirmation.

"I was helping you breathe until I got you to the surface, but I'm all for kissing you anytime you want. That was fucking hot."

My cheeks ignite and my stomach twists, my brain taking a moment to register his words. "Wait, helping me breathe? That was real?"

"Yeah." He holds my gaze, assessing me. "That was real."

"I don't understand. How?" He stares at me, waiting and then it clicks. "You're a merman?" My eyes widen, and I rip my hand from his, an unreasonable sense of betrayal washing over me. Pushing to jump up, I fall back on the sand, bumping against him as my vision blurs.

"Whoa." He reaches out, steadying me. "You still need some time to recover. Give yourself a few minutes."

"But..."

"It's okay, Arie. I know this seems like a lot, but I promise, I'm not going to let anything happen to you."

My mind races, trying to fit the puzzle pieces together, but one question seems to lead to another. Sighing, I give in. "How long was I out?"

"I woke you up a few times during the night to make sure you were okay, but I guess you were out about twelve hours."

"Twelve hours?!"

"You needed it."

I shake my head in disbelief, my hands covering my face. "This is ridiculous. I feel like I'm in an alternate universe."

He shrugs. "You kind of are."

My hands fall to my sides and my mouth drops open as I look around, desperate to understand. "It looks like we're on a beach inside a cave, like the one at the bottom of the cliff."

"Yes, we are, but not quite in the same place we started, although it looks identical. We crossed through an invisible barrier into a hidden world. Look." He tips his head back, gesturing behind him.

I glance over his shoulder seeing vivid colors peeking out from behind the rocks. Although, besides flowers, I can't tell what I'm looking at. "Where are we?"

"That's the town of Pierrecel."

"Where?"

"It's not a town known to most humans."

This is too much. I shake my head in denial. "Humans? What are you talking about Kai? You're not making any sense."

"Calm down Ariana. I promise you're safe. Why don't you come with me, and I'll show you." He holds out his hand, but I don't move. "Either way, I want to get you some water and food. Plus, I'm going to need to find a new phone so I can text my cousins. I left mine on the cliff and I assume yours isn't working anymore."

"Ugh." I frown, pulling my phone out of my pocket. "Maybe we can buy a bag of rice to soak up the moisture."

He laughs, the sound giving me goosebumps. "Rice is not going to work this time, but I am going to need you to get up when you think you're ready." He sets my shoes beside me. "These are pretty dry if you want to put them on."

Grimacing, I mutter, "Thank you. Where are yours?"

I slip them on my feet and tie my laces, Kai not taking his eyes off me. "I'm fine barefoot."

When I'm done, he leans in a little closer, a crooked smile on his face, chipping away at my hesitation. "Please come with me?"

"Fine." With a resigned sigh, I take his hand, my fingers tingling, giving me an overwhelming sense of being safe and warm. Trying to ignore the feeling, I focus on standing. He helps me up and I wobble, still unsteady on my feet.

"You, okay? Need more time?"

"I'll be all right," I answer at the same time holding his hand a little tighter, everything about the moment surreal with a touch of deja-vu, but that's preposterous. Taking another deep breath, I exhale slowly and look into his eyes; the same eyes that could probably lead me into the depths of hell and I'd go willingly. "I'm ready."

"Okay." He nods. Reaching up, he tucks a loose strand of hair behind my ear, his fingers landing on my chin. He leans in and I lick my lips in anticipation, his heated breath tickling my skin. "The next time we kiss, you won't forget a single thing about it. I know I sure as hell won't."

"Kai," I whimper.

I'm about to close the distance when he falls back on his heels with a shake of his head. "Time to go before we get ourselves into trouble."

"I don't mind." My brazen words surprise me. It's like my head and heart made a U-turn in the middle of this conversation. They don't seem to care that I'm completely mystified. Or maybe I'm reconciled to accepting this new existence as long as I'm in it with Kai.

His head falls back in laughter, the sound causing chaos to erupt on my insides. "I'm inclined to agree, but unfortunately, not now." His stomach growls, bringing a bashful grin to his lips. "I need to feed you and I'm hungry too. Let's go eat, and I'll show you around town."

"Sure, I could eat."

Chapter 6

Ariana

I'm not sure if I'm dreaming or not but spending time with Kai in this magical world doesn't seem so bad to me. I don't have to deal with Cleo, and I get to spend the day talking and looking at this sexy man.

Embracing the moment, I spin in a circle, taking in everything around me, Kai's laughter spurring me on. We stroll along the crystal blue water, the saltwater stream widening as we round the rocks, a field of flowers on the other side. The vivid colors are brighter than I could've ever imagined, their sweet floral scent strong and unique.

On our side of the water, buildings and movement come into view, but what I see is not like something I'm used to. A deep purple sand covers the roads, the homes appearing as if they're made of a similar sand, but in all different colors. Bending down, I run my fingers over it, attempting to pick some up, but it's nearly impossible.

"It's not sand like on the beach, this material is more like a colorful, grainy steel, but the texture helps so you don't slip." At that moment, I stumble, catching myself and making him chuckle. "I never said anything about tripping."

"Hey," I warn poking him in his side, not able to hold back my grin.

A woman about five feet, nine inches, with a slim, lithe form, bright blue eyes and pale blue iridescent skin walks by, nodding at Kai. "Who is that?"

"Who or what?" He smirks.

Pursing my lips, I shrug and answer honestly, "Both."

He chuckles. "Did you see her ears?"

I shake my head, glancing back in her direction, noticing her ears poking out of her hair. "They're pointed. Is she an elf?"

"She's a water nymph. There are several that live on this ocean to help protect the water and one of the few entrances into our world. Although, they aren't fighters, they're more healers."

"She's beautiful."

"I guess, but I may be a little biased." His gaze runs over me like a caress, his eyes soft. "You're absolutely stunning."

My face heats and stomach flips. "You've saved my life twice today, I'm sure that doesn't make for me looking at all good."

"Whatever you have to tell yourself, but I know the truth."

His name falls from my lips, my voice reverent. "Kai."

He chuckles and shakes his head as if ridding himself of his thoughts. Moving closer, he looks around, needing a distraction. Pausing, he gestures towards a man and a woman stepping out of a bright yellow and white house, surrounded by flowers and adorned with a wooden sign advertising cookies by the door on our left. "See those two fighting?"

"Yes."

"The man with the bronze skin and golden blonde hair is a sun elf and the woman with the pale skin and silver hair is a moon elf. They fight all the time, but they're also happily married. The whole world knows when they're having a bad day or a good one."

"Really?"

He shrugs. "Well, the extreme days anyway."

"What would that even look like? Storms?"

"I'm sure you'll have a chance to find out." I smile up at Kai, twisting once again. His intense violet orbs pull me in. My breathing picks up its pace. He lifts his hand, trailing it up my jaw, palming my cheek. Without thinking, I lean into it, into him, the feeling warm and comforting. Suddenly, he nods at someone walking by, breaking our stare.

I take the moment to catch my breath and look around at the colorful buildings. It's a little overwhelming, but at the same time I have an odd sense of peace. We walk through a large open courtyard, elves, creatures and people milling about between the homes. "People live here too?" I inquire.

"There's a few, but those people are married to someone from this world. But some of the people you see are not people at all."

"Like you?"

"Some, but there's other species too."

"Like what? Fairies? Trolls? Werewolves?"

"Yeah, plus vampires, griffins and dragons, to name a few, but they all don't live here. Don't worry. Most of the different species have their own communities and kingdoms."

My mouth drops open in shock. "I was joking."

"I'm not, but I promise you're safe here, especially with me." He grins and holds out his hands to the world in front of us, like he's presenting it to me on a platter. "This is the center of town."

Tearing my gaze from him, I slowly spin around. "But it's all houses," I murmur, my confusion evident.

"Yeah, it's a different kind of town. They trade all their goods and services doing what they love. Food, furniture, landscaping, restaurants, and that doesn't even scratch the surface. Basically, it's everything you would see in your world sold out of their homes."

"What about for bigger things? Like something that would take more than one person like construction?"

"Big projects like that, they work together. Everyone is always willing to help. Then on weekends, the entire town meets in the courtyard, over there." He gestures to a massive blue field between two of the homes with a path leading towards it. "It's kind of like a farmer's market of goods and services. Other times, they stop in at one another's homes. A lot of them have signs to show what they have to offer or what they share."

"Like the cookie sign we saw before."

He nods. "Yeah, and some have been here so long, you either know where they are, or you find it by asking around."

"That's incredible. I wish life could be that simple. It's all so beautiful. I can't imagine they're all like this."

"No, but as long as you don't go exploring without me, you shouldn't find yourself in a place you don't want to be."

"I'm not leaving your side."

He smiles, his violet eyes sparkling, the look on his face making my chest tight. "You're taking all of this surprisingly well."

Huffing a laugh, I shrug. "You're right. Honestly, I'm surprising myself, but being here with you feels natural, as if everything is clear for the first time in my life. There's something about you and this town that gives me an odd sense of comfort and I have no idea why. I have these moments where it feels like I've been here before, or that I'm coming home and with you, Kai, it feels like I've known you forever, but that's impossible."

He gives me a tight smile. "Yeah, impossible, but it does feel like I've known you for a long time, Arie."

Biting my lip, I hold back my grin. "It really does, doesn't it? Your cousins talk about you all the time, but it feels like more than that."

"I may have heard your name once or twice over the years too." His lips twitch up in amusement and soon we're both laughing, the atmosphere around us light.

"Thank you for bringing me here."

"You're welcome. I did promise you I would feed you, though, but I still haven't delivered. Want to grab a burger?"

"They have those here?"

He laughs. "Yes, they have burgers here. They also have chicken, hot dogs, pizza and a lot of other good food, but they have things for a very different palette as well. I promise to avoid those places."

Giggling, I urge, "Then, let's grab a burger."

What feels like a permanent smile curves my lips while I stare at him, getting lost in his violet eyes. I've never felt more confident and safe. Maybe it's just me or maybe the man standing beside me giving me a sense of contentment as we walk down the cobblestone streets of Pierrecel has something to do with it. I glimpse at him out of the corner of my eye.

Kai stands tall, still without a shirt, making my mouth water. I can't help but notice others watch him, nodding and smiling as we pass, but I don't blame them. I'm just happy to be here with him.

Glancing at me, he reaches for my hand once again. His touch sends a bolt through my body. "Arie?" he prods, his voice low.

Gasping, I hold his gaze, my breath catching.

"Damn, what are you doing to me?" He licks his lips and gives my hand a gentle tug before spinning me away, laughing as we walk up to a house and through the gate on the side. It feels more like a backyard barbecue than a restaurant and we haven't even sat down.

"Mm," I murmur, inhaling deeply, my stomach growling in anticipation. "It smells good, so good," I emphasize, groaning.

Kai leans down, whispering in my ear, his heated breath eliciting goosebumps, "Moan like that again and I'll be begging you to let me take you right here."

My cheeks flush, my stomach tightens and my juices flow, soaking my underwear without my consent. I'm not one for voyeurism, but man I want him. Knowing he desires me too is what pushes me over the edge.

A man nods at Kai. "Your Ma–"

"Tamon. How are you?" Kai interrupts, grinning wide. "Would I be able to offer you a trade for a meal?"

"I'm happy to provide food for you and the lady."

"Thank you, Tamon."

Kai wraps his arm around me, as if claiming me. He orders for us before we walk over to a picnic table, made of splinter-free wood. Guiding me to sit next to him, he explains, "Someone else might sit down with us. There are different expectations here. If you're sharing a meal in someone's backyard, we're all treated like family and friends. And I'm not about to let anyone but me be the one sitting next to you."

Giggling, my body flames, and my cheeks turn red. "In all the stories I've been told about you, I never heard you were so chivalrous."

"I'm not." He looks into my eyes, his dimple once again making me melt.

Chapter 7

Kai

My gaze remains glued to Arie, watching as she takes the last bite of her burger, her eyes closing as she moans, savoring the flavors. She is going to be the death of me. "Damn, woman. Didn't I warn you about those sexy sounds?"

She blushes a deep shade of red making me chuckle. "Not happening, Kai," she claims. "At least not here," she mumbles under her breath, both of us smirking.

"I'll wear you down."

"So, if you're a merman, why don't you live in the ocean?" She tilts her head up towards me, wiping her hands on her napkin.

"I do. Well, technically, I have two homes, one on the beach and one on the ocean floor."

"What do you mean technically?"

"There are four different places I sleep in, but only two of them are mine."

Her eyes widen. "Only?"

Ignoring her poke, I continue, "You know the beach house we're staying at?"

"Yeah." I nod.

"I stay there when I'm in the human world, but that's more Freddie and Saylor's place than anything. My house on the beach is here in Pierrecel and then I have a place in the water near my family. Although most of the time I'll still crash at my parents' place because it's easier. I have my own room there, but having space is imperative when it comes to my family."

She brightens. "Do you have a big family? Obviously, I know your two cousins, but I'm not sure about the rest. I've always wanted a big family."

"Sort of, but mostly cousins. My mom had a lot of siblings like Freddie and Saylor's mom. I'm not sure if you know, but one of our aunts died when we were young."

Her face falls, showing nothing but genuine empathy making my heart lurch, wanting to pull her into my arms. "I'm so sorry, Kai."

"Thanks. I don't remember much about her, but I thought you would understand." I grind my jaw, watching her close. I haven't really talked about my aunt's death in years. It's still not easy. Plus, my mom's description about what happened to her never ceases to poison my perception.

Her face falls, but she quickly schools her expression, offering me a sad smile. "I do. How did she die? Was it an accident like my parents?"

"No." Shaking my head, I huff a humorless laugh. "She was murdered."

She gasps, her mouth dropping open in shock. Her face pales and she reaches towards me, grabbing my hand and squeezing, causing my chest to tighten. "I'm so sorry, Kai. I can't imagine how difficult that must've been for all of you. Saylor never told me."

"It's not something that's easy to talk about–not for any of us." I pause, anxiously looking around, not sure who might be listening, before bringing my gaze back to Ariana. "Do you want to get out of here?"

"Yeah, I do."

We rise and I nod towards Tamon in appreciation. Before I move, Ariana steps into me, wrapping her arms around my waist, and laying her head on my chest. Surprised, it takes me a moment before my hand falls to her back and I pull her close, resting my cheek on the top of her head. Soon our heartbeats fall into a steady rhythm as if beating as one. I could stand right here with her forever, but I don't want everyone's eyes on us any longer.

Loosening my hold, I gently move her away. I tilt my head down, tenderly brushing my lips over hers, eager to kiss her. Arie's salty, sweet taste seeps into my pores as if she's already becoming a part of me. "Thank you, Ariana."

Her cheeks turn pink, and she smiles, squeezing my heart. "I appreciate you for opening up to me about that, Kai. If you ever need someone to talk to, I'm happy to be here."

"Thanks." I've already shared more than I should, but I don't give a fuck. I have an intense yearning to learn more about her and share every detail about myself. Biting my tongue, I try not to ask too many questions and scare her away. She's not just beautiful, but it's obvious she's smart in the way she talks to me. Her strength and resilience was shining through when she told me about her accident or asked questions about my world.

There's something about her that makes her so easy to talk to. I feel the need to protect her, but how? Will I be able to if she truly is the one?

She moves further back, glancing up at me. Her bright green eyes sparkle, filled with trust and desire, causing my breath to hitch. Fuck. I don't know if I can do this, but I don't want it to end.

Keeping my arm around her shoulders, we stroll down the street side by side, my body craving her more by the second. Her footsteps falter and she lifts her gaze to mine. "Wait, was Atlas really working in a castle?"

Chuckling, I affirm, "Yeah, at the bottom of the ocean."

"Wow," she murmurs in awe and continues walking.

"How about we pick up a new phone so I can text Saylor and Freddie, then we can go back to my place here?" She flushes and I hold my free hand up, jumping in to amend my suggestion. "Arie, I'm not assuming anything. I promise. I'll be the perfect gentleman if that's what you want. I'm just having a lot of fun with you and I want more time with just the two of us before we have to go back to the beach house with everyone else."

She nods and my body relaxes while I breathe a sigh of relief. "We don't have to go back yet. I'm having a good time with you, too and I'd love to see your house."

I grin wide, my mind racing. Looks like I'm going all in. If my mom didn't know about her before, bringing her to my place here almost guarantees she'll find out, but I'm willing to take the chance even if it's only for a few extra minutes with Arie. Eventually, my mom will know soon either way but I'll still do everything I can to maintain our privacy.

However, I have this uneasy feeling in the pit of my stomach telling me that being here not only put Arie in danger, but it set everything in motion. If it's all real, hopefully she won't hate me when she discovers the truth. I don't think I'd survive it.

It's clear there's no turning back now, but I sure as hell need to figure out a way to protect her before it's too late. "Awesome. Let's go."

Chapter 8

Ariana

Kai holds up his phone. "I got in touch with Freddie and Saylor. Saylor kind of freaked out, but they know you're with me and safe."

I wince knowing if the tables were turned and she was gone all night after falling into the ocean, I might have a heart attack. "Thanks."

"No problem. I told them we might be back tomorrow if that's all right with you."

"Sure, but I might need some clean clothes."

He chuckles. "I'm sure we can come up with something." He shows me through his sprawling ranch.

On the right as we walk in, there's a formal living room with a wide fireplace made of a white stone with blue, green and white sea glass embedded into the surface and on the other side of the room, there's a large open doorway leading into a dining room, a massive, white, rectangular, table made of driftwood is placed in the middle with matching chairs. The ones placed on each end remind me of a throne, carved with intricate designs.

To the left, stretching towards the back is a large family room, opening right into a massive country kitchen. Off the main living area, the hallway leads to two bathrooms and a small foyer, the four bedrooms branching off. He has the entire house decorated in accents of blues, purples and greens with seashells, beach glass, driftwood, paintings of the beach, the sea, and unique creatures like I've never seen making me wonder if they're real like the nymph and elves we saw on the way here or the other ones we talked about.

What kind of world am I in and why do I feel so comfortable? Pushing my questions aside, I walk with Kai out back and look around in awe. Sitting on a private cove, the property has its own beach. It's brighter on this side, although, a pale blue shade from the forest darkens the color around the rest of the house like a fence. "It's for both privacy and protection," he explains, shrugging like it's no big deal.

"Who are you?" I ask playfully.

He laughs. "I'm just Kai."

I arch my eyebrows in challenge. "Well, just Kai, I think you're much more than that, but that's enough of an answer for now."

A crooked smile curls his lips as he steps towards me, my heart picking up its pace. "You think you can get more out of me, Ariana?"

"I'm sure willing to try."

His fingers come up, caressing my cheek as he inches closer, his breath mingling with mine. "Go for it. I dare you."

Pushing up on my tiptoes, I press my lips to his. His hand weaves into my hair and he immediately deepens our kiss. My body goes limp, curving into his touch. His tongue slips into my mouth, meeting mine, licking and twisting together, my entire body coming alive, tingling with anticipation. "Kai," I moan, pressing my body into his, ready to jump him right here on his beach.

He pulls back, breathless, leaving me slightly stunned. "Not here, let's go inside." My brows pinch together in confusion. "You never know who's in the water, even on private property."

"Oh." My eyes widen and I quickly step away, stumbling back.

He laughs, grabbing me around the waist to steady me before I fall. "You need a personal bodyguard to keep you safe and upright."

I giggle as we walk inside his massive home. "Gee, thanks. I've never been great on my feet. My mom signed me up for ballet class when I was seven thinking it would help, but that didn't last long."

He smirks. "I'm trying to imagine you in a pink tutu."

My head falls back in laughter. Focusing, I look at him with a small shake of my head, my lips curling upwards. "You're too much."

"And you're the most beautiful woman I've ever seen."

My heart clenches, and my breathing picks up its pace. "Kai."

He threads his fingers into my hair, his violet orbs captivating me as he looks into my eyes. "I want you, Ariana, more than my next breath, but I can't make you any promises right now. Please tell me we're on the same page here."

"Believe it or not, I had a crush on you before I even met you. And after the last two days, I know I want you too," I proclaim, my confidence unwavering.

"You had a crush on me?"

Ignoring him, I continue, "I don't need promises when I don't know where either of us will be in a couple months."

A smile lights up his face. He tips his head down, brushing his mouth over mine. His tongue slips out, running along my lips. He kisses me soft and slow making me whimper. Sliding his hands down my back, leaving goosebumps, he grabs my ass, lifting me up. Reflexively, I wrap my legs around his waist, my arms looping around his neck. His mouth moves over mine in a perfect rhythm.

He walks me backwards, while I'm unable to focus on anything but him.

Carefully, he lowers me onto his bed, his kiss remaining tender while his hands begin to roam over my clothes. I've never wanted someone so much. My skin tingles, desperate to feel his skin on mine as if his body is calling out to me like a siren's song. Needing more, I push him back, gasping for breath, insisting, "There's too much between us."

He stands and I follow, pulling my dress over my head and dropping it on the floor, standing in nothing but dark green lace panties. His eyes widen on my bare breasts and his breath catches. "Damn."

Slowly, he moves towards me, and I step back, smiling mischievously. "Shorts first."

Grinning, he steps out of his shorts, his hard length popping free. I lick my lips as he stalks towards me, backing me towards the bed. Reaching for me, his fingers slip into the sides of my underwear, tugging them down my legs, and dropping them to the floor. His breathing picks up its pace as his gaze slowly travels every part of my body, giving me goosebumps and perking my nipples. "You're absolute perfection."

I sit down on the edge of the bed and scoot back. Kai lays down next to me, his fingers running over my lips, trailing down my neck and over my chest. My heart races as his hand finds my breasts, squeezing my already pert nipples one by one, followed by the brush of his lips. I arch my back, trying to get closer while my hands frantically roam his body, wanting to touch every inch of his skin. Obliging my silent request, he sucks my breast into his mouth.

"Kai," I moan, urging him on, my pussy already throbbing.

Moving up, he covers my mouth with his, our kisses more desperate, tongues fighting for dominance. His hand slides down my side, and between my legs, gliding his fingers between my folds. My head falls back, breaking our kiss with a whimper.

"Fuck, you're so wet for me." His finger slips inside, followed by another, with his thumb pressing against my nub, eliciting a guttural moan.

"We've had a day full of foreplay. I don't want to wait anymore, Kai. My body is vibrating. I'm ready. Please."

I reach for his thick shaft, running my fingers along the growing length before attempting to wrap my fingers around his cock. With one squeeze, he grunts. "Arie, if you're letting me inside you, our first time needs to be just that because I'm more than primed, but I promise you'll get your chance to explore as much as you want. We have all night."

Enjoying the moment, I let go, allowing him to lead. Reaching towards his nightstand, he opens the drawer and pulls out a condom, ripping it open and rolling it on. Hovering over me, he lines up at my entrance and looks me in the eyes. "Are you sure this is what you want?"

"Yes, Kai. I want you. Please." I curl one leg around his back, urging him towards me.

His lips find mine, kissing me hard, and relentless, as I feel him entering me. With one quick thrust, he's inside making us both gasp. He pauses his movements, letting me adjust, but my body rages, burning for our connection. My insides are swollen with desire and in this moment, it feels like nothing but Kai can help satisfy my hunger.

I arch towards him and he answers me with his body. Pulling out, he drives back in, our hips colliding, skin slapping, and his cock hitting the spot at the back of my pussy over and over again. His thrusts soon come faster, harder, deeper. I wrap my other leg around him, dragging my fingers up and down his back and digging into his firm muscles. My breathing becomes uneven, while my body feels like it's flourishing, igniting, and scorching.

A guttural sound echoes in the room, but I'm not sure if it's him or me. I just know I need more, and he gives it to me. "Kai, I'm going to…" I trail off breathless, focusing on the sensations consuming my body. My orgasm starts in my fingers and toes, building towards my core and coiling deep in my belly. "Ah…" My body begins to vibrate, completely on fire, barely a moment before my insides clench, squeezing his cock and wracking my body.

As I start to come down from my extreme high, he grunts, "Fuck!" His movements become erratic as he thrusts faster and harder.

My body reacts, another orgasm coming on almost instantly. Feeling like every part of me is burning up, my legs tighten around him as he plunges deep inside me. My body pulses, milking his cock as he drives again and again, pausing at the hilt before he collapses on top of me with a harsh exhale.

We lay together breathless, overwhelmed by the reaction my body seems to have with this man. Everything about this experience surreal.

"You, okay?" he asks, sliding off of me. Laying on his side, he props his head on his hand and keeps his other arm draped across my waist while looking down at me, waiting for a response.

"Yeah, but I'm wondering how I went from spending a week with my best friend at the beach to a night of hot sex with you."

"Just hot sex?" He arches his eyebrows in challenge. "That was so much more than that. Maybe the best sex you ever had?"

A giggle falls from my lips. "It was something all right."

He rolls over me, pinning my hands above my head and holding me down with his hips. "I'm positive that was fantastic and if you agree with me, you just may get more."

I make a face, and he sucks my nipple, causing my eyes to roll back in my head as I arch towards him. "Okay, you win. It was the best sex you ever had." Still sucking, his fingers slip between my legs, making me groan in pleasure. "You, me, we...best sex ever," I stammer breathlessly.

It's true, but I'm not about to think about that right now, let alone sincerely admit it to him.

Chapter 9

Ariana

My eyes flutter open, glancing over at the sexy man lying next to me. He's still here. A smile tugs at my lips remembering his touch and sweet, steamy kisses over every inch of my body. That man can kiss and his tongue–mmm–is pure bliss.

"You're awake," he murmurs, the deep sound of his voice rumbling over me and giving me chills.

"I am, but I can't move."

He chuckles. Reaching over, he gently trails his fingers down my arm and over my belly. "I bet I can make you move."

A smile tugs at the corners of my mouth. "I think you've proven over and over again that you can make me do a lot of things."

"I'm happy to say the same about you."

A soft sigh escapes my mouth. "But I guess we should go back to the beach house today."

"Should we really? I kinda like what we have going here." He pushes up, brushing his lips over my shoulder and trailing up my neck. "My cousins sure as hell won't miss me."

"Oh my gosh, your cousins. I don't know why I didn't think about it before, but if your cousins are Saylor and Freddie, are they mermaids too?"

He drops back against the mattress with a harsh exhale. "Sorta."

"What is it with you and half answers?" I laugh.

Smirking, he shrugs. "Well, Freddie would be offended knowing you called him a mermaid."

"You know what I mean." Playfully, I poke him in his side, hurting my finger. "Ow."

Chuckling softly, he grabs my finger, kissing it. "Careful. I'm harder than I look." My stomach twists and he sighs. "Arie, I'm not trying to hide anything from you. I just think since Saylor is your best friend and you've known her a long time, that's a conversation you should have with her. I'm not stepping on anyone's toes."

I pinch my lips tightly together and sigh. "That's fair, but now I don't know if I want to go back."

"Sounds good to me." Leaning in he presses his lips to my neck.

Giggling, I insist, "It doesn't have anything to do with you or sex." Scowling, he drops back to the bed making me laugh harder. Catching my breath, I explain, "That's a weird conversation to have with everyone there."

"Sure, it can be, but she probably already has an idea you know since I dove in the water after you. Besides, I'm sure you could find some time for just you and Saylor to go somewhere and talk if you really want."

"Yeah, but now I also don't want to miss any time with you. I live with Saylor, but I don't know if or when I'll see you again." No matter how much I'd like to. "Are you sticking around the entire week?"

"I was planning on it. I promised my cousins I'd celebrate their birthdays with them and now that also means I get to be there to enjoy yours."

"Then what happens after next week?"

"What do you mean? Are you asking what we are Ariana?" He arches his eyebrows, a smile tugging at the corners of his lips.

"No. No. I know what I agreed to. I'm asking about your plans."

He frowns. "I have to go back to work for my family, at least for now."

"Don't look too excited about it."

"I'm not, but it's fine."

"I can't believe I'm saying this, but I wish I could come with you to see your world under the ocean, your home there."

He glances at me with a broad smile. "You do?"

"I've never felt calm around water, but for some reason, here with you, I do." He gives me a look I can't quite decipher. "I promise I'm not a stalker."

"That's what all stalkers say." He smirks.

"Well, it's not like I could stalk you even if I wanted to without your help."

He chuckles. "I guess that's true. You can, you know."

"Can what? Stalk you?"

His head falls back as he bursts out laughing. He meets my gaze, his eyes sparkling. "You can come with me into the ocean to see my home."

My eyes widen in surprise. "What? How?"

"With me you can do anything, and I believe you have the power to do so much more than you realize."

"Well, thanks for believing in me, Kai, but this isn't like me going home to meet your parents. I don't breathe under water."

"You did before."

"Because I fell in and almost died, but you saved me and had to breathe for me. You can't swim around the ocean with me attached to your lips."

He chuckles. "Why not?"

"Kai," I mutter in warning, narrowing my eyes.

His voice turns soft. "Ariana, do you trust me?"

"Trust you? I barely know you."

"You sure about that?" Reaching for my hand, he entwines are fingers together and squeezes. "Don't you feel that connection between us? To me it feels like fireworks exploding and at the same time a soft blanket cocooning us to keep us safe and warm. It feels like we've known each other forever and not just because of stories we've been told. We're connected in a way that I can't explain. Don't you feel it, Arie?" He stares at me, his violet eyes pleading as if eager for it to be true.

Gulping down the lump in my throat, I nod. "Yeah, I do feel something different with you, but that doesn't mean I can breathe under water."

"All you have to do is trust me and we'll figure out the rest together. Come swimming with me. Please."

My heart skips a beat, suddenly terrified, but it has nothing to do with the ocean. Kai leans over and brushes his lips over mine, giving me an encouraging smile, the simple gesture calming me once again.

"I won't let anything happen to you, Arie."

My stomach twists into knots as I search his gaze, but I believe him. Finally, I nod in agreement, shocking myself.

"Okay. I'm putting my trust in you. Let's go, Kai."

Chapter 10

Kai

My heart hammers, and my hands shake while I attempt to remain calm for Ariana. I'm anxious, but she can't know. It would only make her more uneasy. I'm not about to let her back away from me. If there's a chance we can do this together, I've got to take it. "You've got this," I claim, watching her nervous gaze. "With a lover's kiss, I give you breath, but even then, I won't leave your side. It's a little bit of ocean magic."

"Why couldn't you do that before?"

"Because you weren't conscious and couldn't make a decision on your own, but you are now. We can do this together."

"Are you sure?"

I kiss her again. "Arie, I promise you'll be safe with me. Just try to relax."

She exhales slowly and nods. "Okay. Let's do this before I chicken out."

"Okay." I put one hand on her heart and the other around her back, holding her close as I look into her eyes. Taking a deep breath, I kiss her soft and slow, releasing my breath into her lungs and gently pulling us under the water together. Her body goes taut, but soon relaxes in my arms. Moments later, I pull back and watch her close, still holding her hands.

Her eyes widen and she gasps as if struggling to breathe. I cradle her face in my hands and hold her gaze, watching as she settles and begins to breathe on her own. She looks down, a shimmering teal green tail flipping up behind her.

A smile lights up her face. "How is this possible?"

My heart thunders at the reality in front of me, a grin tugging at my lips. "I knew it was you. I could feel it."

"What are you talking about?"

"You're the lost mermaid."

Her eyebrows draw down in confusion. "What?"

"Now that we've been together, giving you my breath puts a crack in the curse and helps you see who you truly are."

"Curse? You're talking in riddles."

"Kai, you found her," my mother says from behind me.

My body stiffens and I spin around with wide eyes. "Mom? What are you doing here?"

"Can't a mother welcome her son home?" she taunts, her voice sickly sweet. "Especially when he comes with such a wonderful gift."

I shake my head, moving in front of Arie. "She's not a gift."

"Kai, what's going on?" Ariana whispers in my ear.

"Ariana, this is my mom," I mutter, glaring at my mother.

Arie smiles, showing her manners. "Oh, it's nice..."

I hold up my hand to stop her. "No, please don't go near her."

Her eyebrows draw down in confusion. "Kai?"

My mother lets out a dark laugh. "Did you not tell her the story, my boy?"

"Story? What story?" Ariana questions, clearly baffled, glancing at me.

"The story of the lost mermaid princess. Her parents claimed she died at sea, but I knew better. You are the lost princess."

Ariana gasps, shaking her head in disbelief, her wide eyes flying to mine. "No, I'm not a princess."

"You're not fit to be one, I'll give you that." She scrunches up her face in disgust as she looks her over from head to toe. "Unfortunately, your family tree says otherwise, but now that you're here, I'm going to change the future."

"Stay away from her, Mom!"

Ignoring me, she continues, glaring at Arie, "I knew your parents were hiding you after my sister tried to murder your mom. Your dad killed my sister, you know."

My mind races, searching for a way out of this mess. I should've known better than to bring her into this world without setting up protection first. What am I going to do?

Arie shakes her head, vehemently negating, "No. That's not true. My dad would never kill anyone. He was a good man."

She slithers closer to Arie, staring her down, her tone, menacing. "Oh, my dear, he did and when attempts were made on your life years later, they hid you away, and during a horrendous storm, they gave you to a family of humans, trying to convince everyone else you didn't survive. Am I right?"

Ariana shakes her head, tears of denial marring her cheeks. I move to get back in front of her, desperate to protect her, but my mother's security guards stop me, pinning my arms and tail behind my back.

Squirming wildly, I demand, "Let me go!"

Completely disregarding me, my mother continues, "My sisters and I wanted revenge on your family but every time, something or someone stopped us. Then, when you were born early, along with the most powerful prophecy in our history, you stole our reign once again." She scoffs. "We weren't going to stand for that. So, you, Ariana, became our new target. At least I was able to find you and put a curse on you after your parents hid you away. Because of me they had to settle with leaving you with the humans."

"Kai?" Arie questions, her voice cracking.

"Oh, don't look at him, honey, he can't help. In fact, he was the one who was tasked with bringing you to me."

"What?" She gasps, her eyes going wide like saucers, flicking back and forth between my mother and me.

"Arie, it's not what you think," I scream, frantic.

My mother cackles, the sound turning my stomach. "No, it's so much worse. He was meant to seduce you which would eventually help give us back our powers and it looks like he succeeded."

"No!" I shake my head in denial, struggling to get free. "That's not true. I really like her!" Focusing on Ariana, I insist, "I really like you, Arie. Everything that happened with us was real. Don't believe her."

"You think that matters?" My mother scoffs making my blood boil. "You sentenced her the moment you met. After all, the curse I put on Ariana years ago to suppress her powers and to connect her with you was about to wear off." My mother laughs, sending chills down my spine. "The princess's powers would strengthen between her twenty-fourth and twenty-fifth year and her connection to you would be lost. But that's all changed now, and I have you to thank for that *Prince* Kai."

Shit. Reality settles over me. The subtle taste I couldn't decipher when I first kissed Arie was remnants from my mother's spell.

"No!" I deny at the same time, Ariana's green eyes veer to me, staring at me with bitter betrayal. "I'm crazy about you, Ariana. I would never hurt you."

"Oh, but you did, my son. And now Ariana and her family will finally pay for what they did and we will take full power of the sea into our family's hands where it belongs."

Maintaining my gaze on Arie, my chest tightens, aching, while helplessly watching as pain fills her eyes and overflows. "Arie, please," I plead, defenselessly.

"My Queen?" Cleo swims up, all eight of her legs out and shaking with delight, fueling my anger. Her mom was an octopus and her father a merman, making her a hybrid. "Yes, it worked. I knew pushing you over the edge would set you off. Now we can be together again, Kai."

Glaring at Cleo, I seethe, gritting through my teeth, "I'm not getting back together with you, ever."

She laughs, kissing me with no way for me to break free, guards still holding me back. I clench my jaw confident she's trying to hurt Arie and I pray she doesn't believe any of this. She breaks the kiss and pulls back, giving Ariana a mischievous grin.

"Don't believe this, Arie. Please. You know I only want you."

"I don't know what I believe."

Her quiet confession breaks my heart. I only pray she'll forgive me. Needing to give her some hope, I blurt out, "Your dad is still alive."

A soft gasp falls from her lips. "My dad?"

My mom startles, quickly schooling her features. Her head falls back in laughter, as if the thought is ridiculous. But we both know she imprisoned him after killing her mother. "I killed both her parents long ago."

I shake my head. "That's a lie. Your dad is alive."

Ariana bobs in the water, stunned, surrounded by more of my mother's guards. She wipes away the tears in her eyes, her body stiffening. "We're meant to be together, Ariana. I know it. Please, believe me. I will save you."

She shakes her head, huffing a humorless laugh. "How am I supposed to believe anything you say, Kai? This time I'll save myself." The guards drag Ariana away, with her head held high and obliterating my heart.

Attempting to yank my hands and fins free, I yell, "Please, don't hurt her! Where are you taking her?"

"Settle down, Kai. We're not going to hurt her–yet. But after she produces your heir, well, then all bets are off."

"It will be a cold day in hell before that happens. I wore a condom every time I was with her."

She tilts her head to the side, giving me a look in mock sympathy. "Oh, you mean those things in your nightstand at your house? I may have had someone break in when I knew you were going to the beach house and make sure those didn't work."

My heart plummets. "What the actual fuck?"

"Thanks, Cleo." She nods at my ex, glancing anxiously in my direction.

"Get the fuck out, Cleo," I grit through my teeth, focusing on my mother.

"Kai," Cleo begs, holding her hand out towards me.

My head snaps to her and I growl, "I said get the fuck out!"

A shrill scream exits her mouth, but she spins around and does as I asked. "Do you have to manipulate everything about my life?"

"Well, I knew I couldn't depend on you not to fall for the girl and I wouldn't let that happen. We can't keep her around if we want the power to pass onto the rest of us and not just you. Our family is due to not only get our full powers back, but the kind of control an heir from the two of you would produce was already written in the stars. You can't stop destiny, but that doesn't mean we can't guide it in the right direction."

"And you're that direction?"

"I will be the *thing's* grandmother after all. Your heir would make our family unstoppable. We wouldn't only rule this king-dom, we could rule them all. Don't you want that kind of influence, Kai?"

Not bothering to answer, knowing it will only get me in trouble, I demand, "Tell them to let me go, *Mother*."

Slithering closer to me, she glares down at me. "Do as I tell you to, Kai. I would hate to be forced to throw my own son in the dungeons, but I will do whatever is necessary to finally get what we deserve."

Gritting my teeth, I hold her stare, remaining silent. Heaving a sigh as if I'm the problem, she waves her hands dismissively, the guards releasing me. Spinning around, I swim away, desperate to get as far away from her as possible so I can think.

First, I have to find Ariana and get her out of here. Then, I will find a way for her to forgive me. I just hope she's not pregnant because if she is, we're all screwed.

"I'm coming for you Arie. I promise."

The Prophecy

Eighteen Years Ago...

Off the coast of Pierrecel beneath the blue ocean waters, the tensions were rising amongst the sea life. Royalty remained divided between mermaids and mermen, sea witches and sea warlocks, each holding their own pieces of the ocean throughout the world.

When families started crossing and new breeds were created, one royal family attempted to take the reins, wanting to control everything beneath the surface, hungry for power. The matriarch of this family started a battle. The feud ended in her demise, by a human prince and his mermaid princess trying to protect their family as well as the people and creatures of land and sea.

The human prince and his mermaid princess soon became the king and queen of both their kingdoms. Their survival ignited a war.

After the birth of their daughter, a new prophecy was declared by the Gods, wanting to restore peace in all the kingdoms. Their daughter's powers would strengthen between her 24th and 25th year. The girl, her future love and their children would become the most powerful creatures in the sea, making them the royalty of all oceans by her 25th birthday.

Threatened, repeated attempts were made on the child's life, but the king and queen kept their princess safe. Until an act of revenge cursed the child, taking away her fin and her power, leaving her human, vulnerable, and one day inexplicably drawn to one of her own, but that wouldn't last forever.

The king and queen took their young princess to the surface living on a boat while they searched for solutions, until they were once again attacked as a storm started brewing. A battle ensued and soon an inferno took hold of their floating safe haven. Lightning and fire lit up the sky, their daughter falling overboard. The treacherous waves rose and crashed tearing them further apart as they fought against their enemies for survival of the future.

As the rain slowed and the waves began to rest, nothing but smoke and ash remained. After months of searching, the king and queen returned to their castle at the bottom of the sea without their princess, distraught. But their war was not over.

Investigations continued year after year, looking for the lost princess to no avail. Accusations of betrayal and deceit were thrown in every direction, speculating if the lost princess were alive, possibly hidden in an unknown realm to maintain her safety, or truly dead. When the king and queen disappeared without a trace fifteen years later, the gossip regarding the royal family only heightened, while other families continued to fight for control.

As the years passed, knowing the curse bestowed upon the lost princess would soon dissipate, many wondered if she might return to claim her throne with or without a prince by her side and fulfill the prophecy of the Gods. Deprived of her, someone else could take power and the battles for control would continue without amity leaving the kingdoms on land and sea in pandemonium.

But with the return of the lost princess, the fight for her love could become a feud for power and the uncertainty of whether there will be chaos or peace.

To Be Continued...

Acknowledgements

This time, the first thank you needs to go to Danielle, an incredible author and friend who encouraged me to step out of my comfort zone and embrace the challenge of romantasy. I had been a swimmer most of my life and being a mermaid is something I definitely dreamed of growing up. I loved every minute of diving into this story and I have the continuation already coming together.

As always, thank you to my family for being my biggest support and cheerleaders, followed closely by my friends.

Thank you to all the fellow authors that were part of the charity anthology, Once Upon a Forsaken Love where this story originated. It was an honor to be a part of this incredible project and all the money we raised for the children's hospital.

Dina, Thank you for pushing me with editing the story. I'm truly grateful for you.

Thank you to Author Kris Woods for the beautiful artwork and design for the cover. I appreciate you!

Thanks to all my Beta readers, my ARC team, my street team and my fans. I wouldn't be able to keep writing and sharing my stories without each and every one of you. THANK YOU!

Other Books by

Nikki A Lamers

<u>The Unforgettable Series</u>

Unforgettable Summer
Unforgettable Nights
Unforgettable Dreams
Unforgettable Memories
Unforgettable One
Unforgettable Mistakes
An Unforgettable December

<u>Mending Shattered Hearts</u>

Breaking Cycles
The War is Over
Breaking Barriers

<u>Home</u>

Dreams Lost and Found
Finding Home

<u>Piper Falls: Station 28</u>

(Interconnected Stand Alone Series)

Leave of My Duty

<u>Love Canyon: Blind Date with a #BOOK-BOYFRIEND</u>

(Interconnected Stand Alone Series)

Blind Date with a #FORMERPLAYER

Connect with the Author

Official Author Website

www.nikkialamersauthor.com

Linktree for All Author Links

https://linktr.ee/NikkiALamersauthor

About the Author

Award Winning Author, Nikki A Lamers grew up in Wisconsin and lived in Florida for a few years before ending up on Long Island in New York where she now lives with her husband and their two children. She writes mostly spicy contemporary and new adult romance, many times incorporating tough health, wellness, and life issues. With her public health background, she loves diving deep into her characters and seeing how some of the tough issues can impact an individual and their relationships.

Recently she has expanded her author catalog with romantic suspense, romantasy and paranormal romance, while maintaining her roots. Writing, reading, coffee, chocolate, and at times a good drink are all she wants alongside her friends and family. Since meeting her husband, they enjoy spending time in Maine and exploring different places, meeting new people, and always crafting her next story. For her other job she freelances as a script writer, advisor, and supervisor on and off set, hoping to one day see a story of her own on screen.

A person with blonde hair wearing a green sweater Description automatically generated